I0960360

Rumple Buttercup

RuMPLe ButteRcuP

a story of bananas, belonging,
and being yourself

written and illustrated
by

Matthew Gray GuBler

Random House 🏠 New York

Copyright © 2019 by Matthew Gray Gubler

All rights reserved. Published in the United States by Random House Children's Books, a division of Penguin Random House LLC, New York.

Random House and the colophon are registered trademarks of Penguin Random House LLC.

Visit us on the web!
rhcbooks.com

Educators and librarians, for a variety of teaching tools, visit us at RHTeachersLibrarians.com

Library of Congress Cataloging-in-Publication Data is available upon request.

ISBN 978-0-525-64844-4 (trade) — ISBN 978-0-525-70763-9 (lib. bdg.) — ISBN 978-0-525-70762-2 (ebook)

MANUFACTURED IN CHINA

10 9 8 7 6 5 4 3 2 1

First Edition

for all the Rumples
everywhere

Chapter

1

Once upon a time,
Long ago and far away
in a tiny town beneath
a purple peaked
pine tree ...

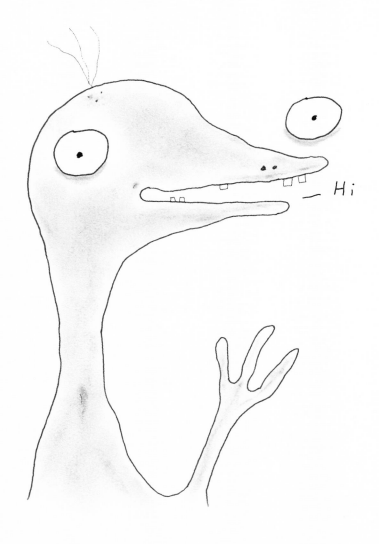

there lived a monster
NAMed Rumple Buttercup

He Had...

5 crooked teeth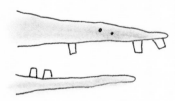

3 strands of hair

Green skin

And his left foot was slightly bigger than his right

He was weird

And so Rumple worried
that if anyone ever saw
him they would...

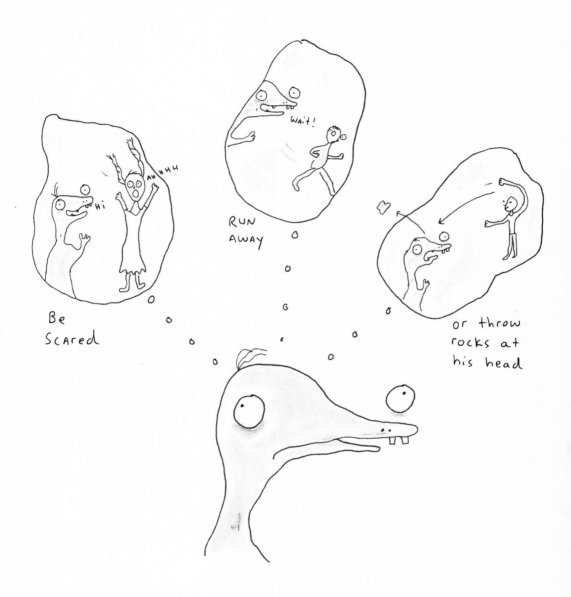

So he spent his entire
life hiding underground
in a rain drain right by
a garbage can in the
middle of town

where no one would ever
see him

But where he could still see
them. Laughing and playing,
Singing and dancing, Walking
dogs and jumping rope

But most of all...

Not Being weird

Living underground wasn't All
bad, though. Rumple made the
most of it and had a nice little
home he decorated with old
garbage he found in the can
outside

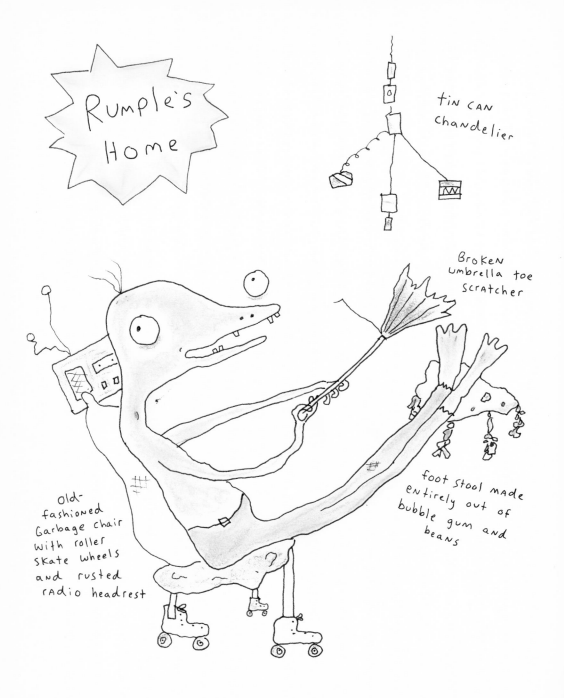

Rumple's Home

tin can chandelier

Broken umbrella toe scratcher

foot stool made entirely out of bubble gum and beans

Old-fashioned Garbage chair with roller skate wheels and rusted radio headrest

there he lived
DAY After dAy
weeK After weeK
year After yeAR

SO MUCH TIME

Alone

So one day he reached in the garbage
can and took...

2 lollipops

A piece of chewed
gum

3 strands of
spaghetti

Some melted
licorice rope

A petrified pretzel

A handful of
candy corn

and created...

Candy Corn Carl

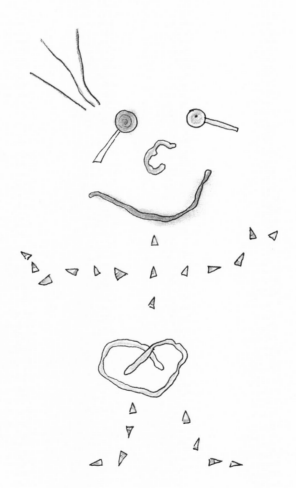

Even though he was just a bunch of old candy that Rumple had glued to the wall, Candy Corn Carl was Rumple's best friend in the world and Rumple would talk to him for hours a day.

What have you been up to, Carl?

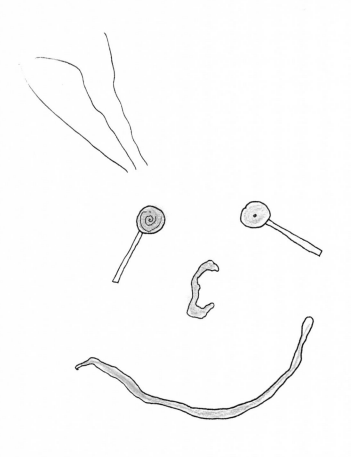

But CarL Never Replied

O.K. well, HANG in there, Carl Get it?

"HANG" in there cause you're hung on the wall *

* If Carl was real he probably would have liked that joke but since he was a bunch of candy stuck to a wall he just stared

When Rumple wasn't building
stuff out of garbage or
talking to Carl he would
listen to the voices above
ground and pretend
they were talking to
him

⊿ ⧊ ⊿

With his eyes shut really
tight it was as if he
was part of all the fun
happening above

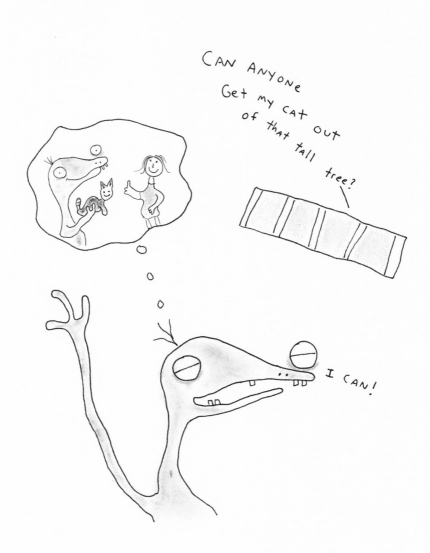

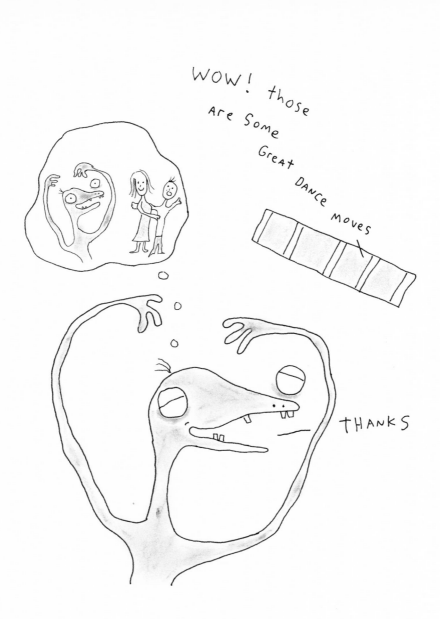

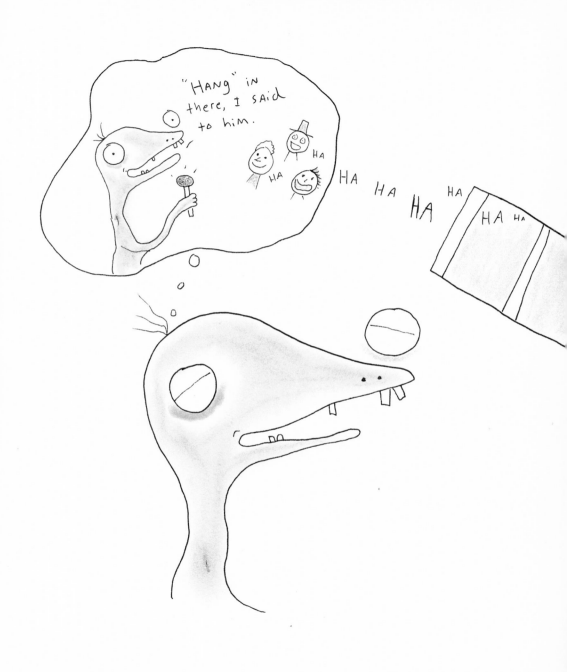

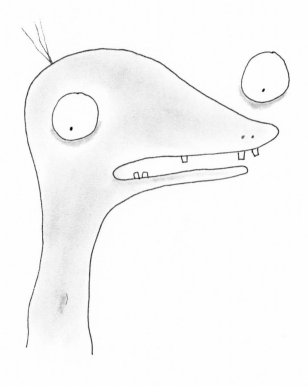

But when he opened his eyes
he would remember that it was
All just a dream and no one
was ever talking to him

Sometimes at Night if
the moon wasn't too bright
and if Rumple was feeling
adventurous he would go
above ground with the help
of a very simple disguise

RumpLe's Above Ground
disguise instructions

Step 1

Get a banana peel out of the garbage can

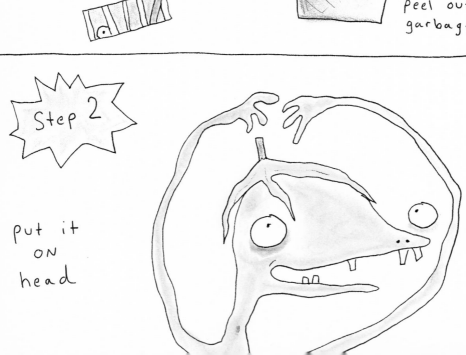

Step 2

put it on head

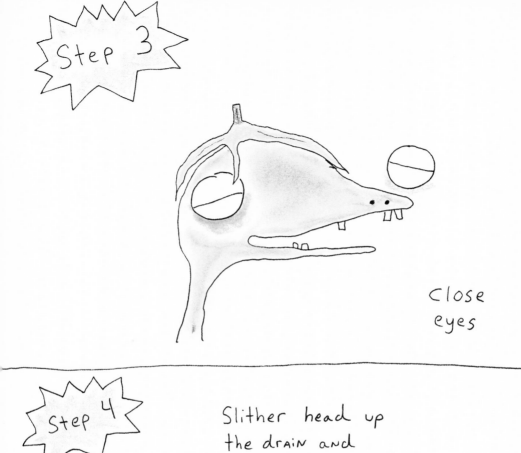

Close
eyes

Slither head up
the drain and
sit very very
still

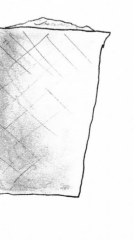

Lying Quietly by the
garbage can No one would
Notice him and if anyone
Saw him they would just
think he was a pile
of trash

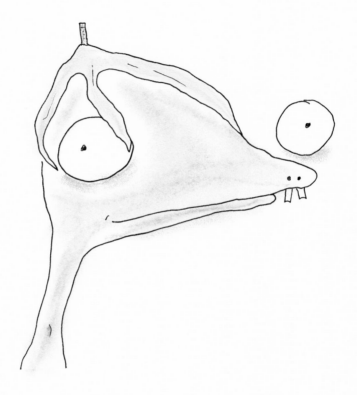

Hidden under his banana peel
Rumple almost felt like he
was normal

Year after year with
his eyes shut tight he
would feel the breeze
of the changing seasons

In October he could
hear the crunching
leaves and almost
taste the apple
cider

In December he would hum along with the passing carolers

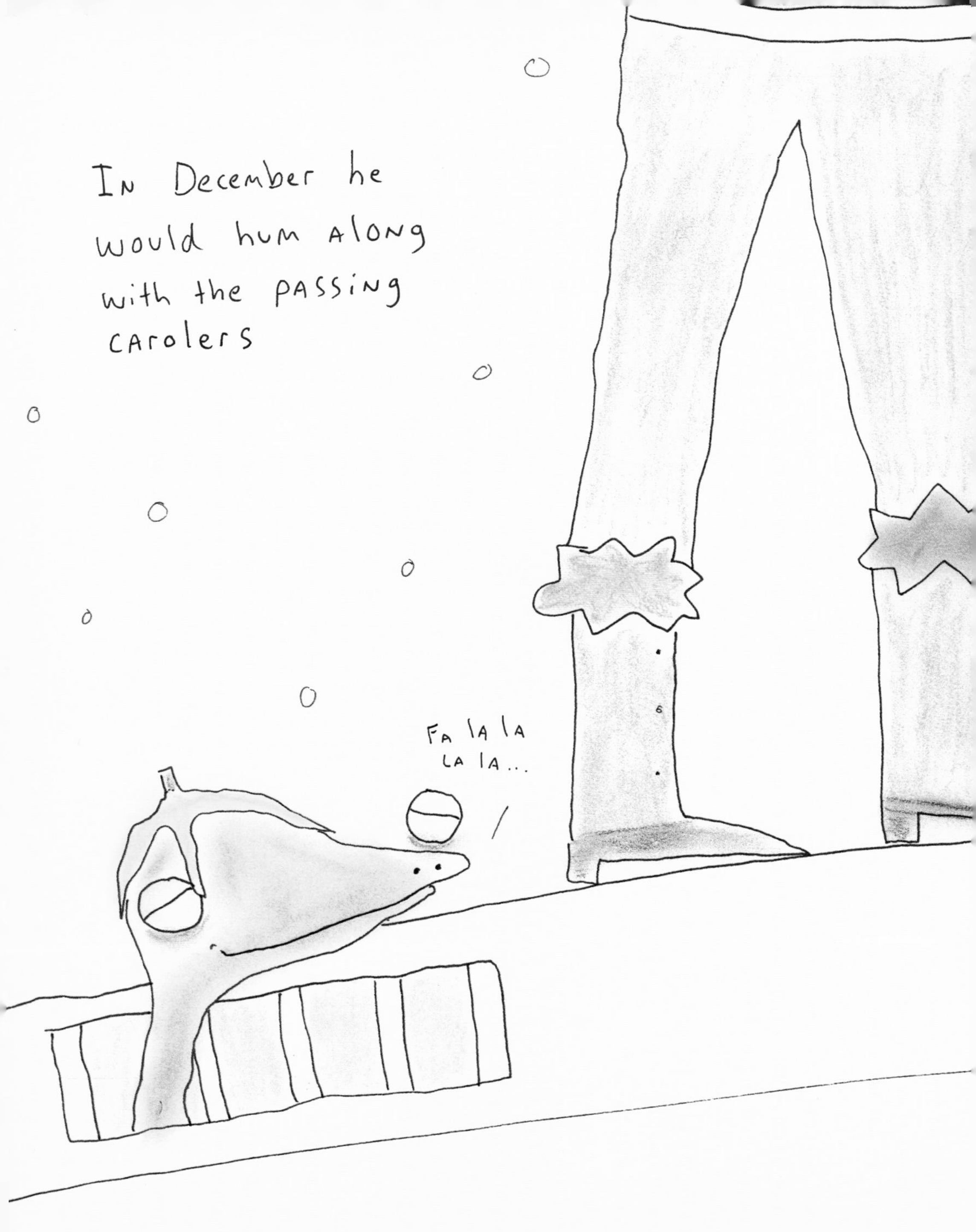

And in July he could imagine the Beautiful fireworks

But at the end of
each night he was
always reminded
that...

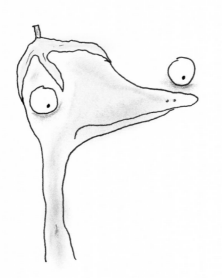

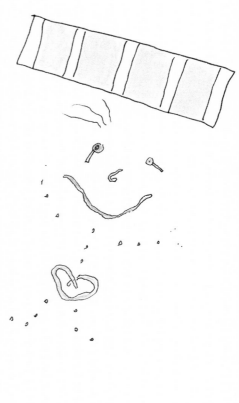

He was still all alone

Chapter
2

The leaves were turning green, which meant that Rumple's favorite day was fast approaching

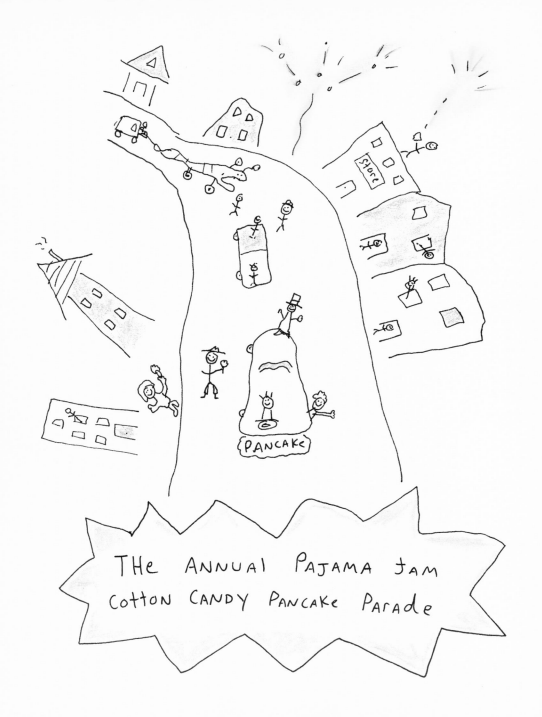

THE ANNUAL PAJAMA JAM
COTTON CANDY PANCAKE PARADE

On the 17th Saturday
of summer everyone in
town would wake up
late, keep their pajamas
on, and march down
the center of town
singing and dancing and
lighting fireworks and
laughing while eating
Giant bushels of cotton
candy pancakes

YAYYY!

Rumple loved this day
most of all because it
was the ONE day of
the year that he could
actually go out in
the daylight

With all of the noise and
commotion no one would
ever notice him...

As long as he had his
disguise

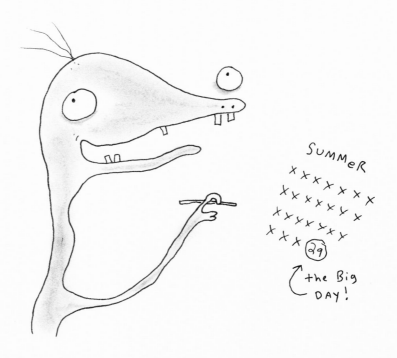

SUMMER

x x x x x x x
x x x x x x x
x x x x x x x
x x x 29 x x x

↳ the Big
   DAY!

AFter a whole year of
waiting the day was Almost
here

the night before, Rumple
was so excited he
could hardly sleep

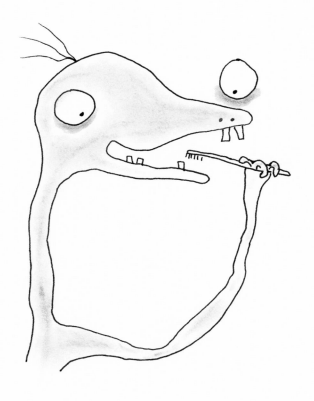

He woke up early the next
morning, brushed his 5
crooked teeth

combed his 3 wispy
hairs

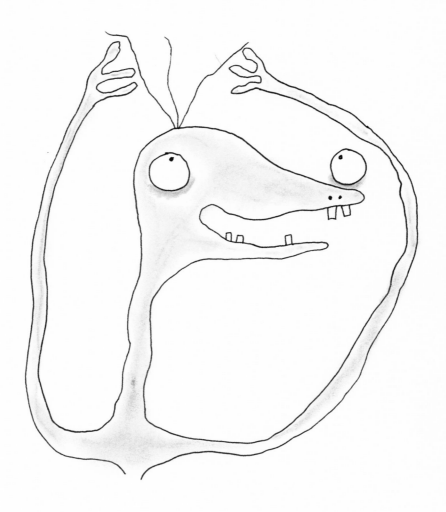

And slowly, carefully
slithered his long green
hand up the rain drain
to find a banana
peel

the garbage can was
empty!

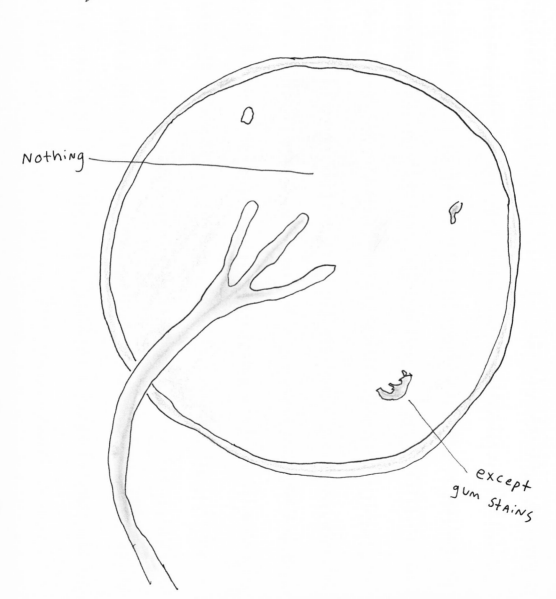

there WAS NO

BANANA PeeL !

"Oh NO!" thought Rumple...
"I'm going to miss the
PAJAMA JAM PANCAKE
parade"

"I can't go Above ground without
my disguise or people will
think I'm weird"

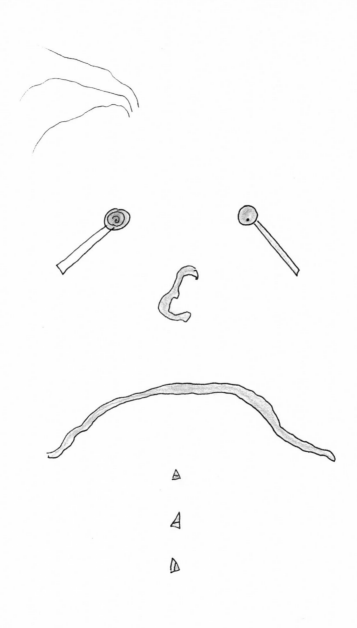

So he lowered his
head ...

And cried

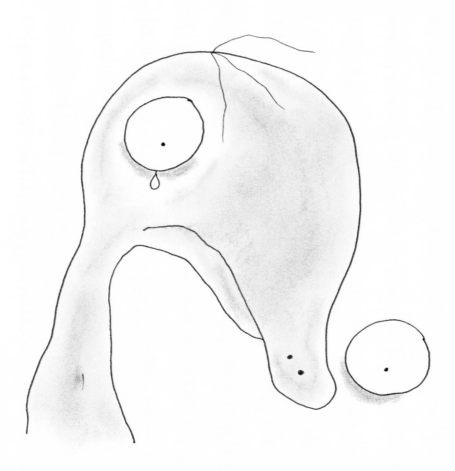

And cried

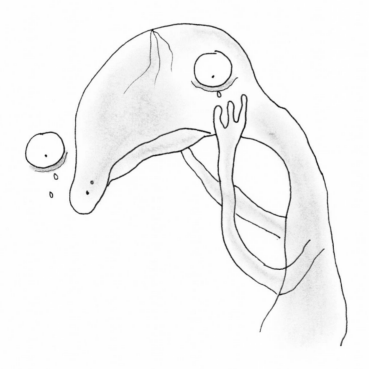

And cried some more

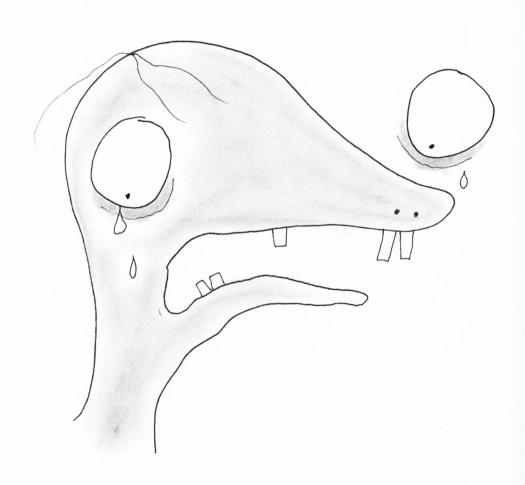

And that is when
he heard it...

Chapter
3

Aren't you going to watch the Parade this Year?

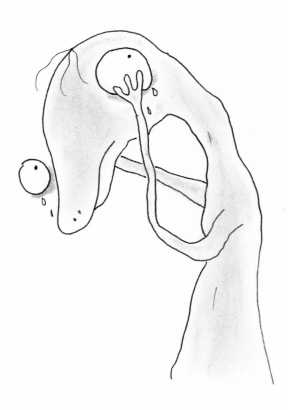

Rumple couldn't believe it! WAS Candy Corn Carl finally talking After All these years?

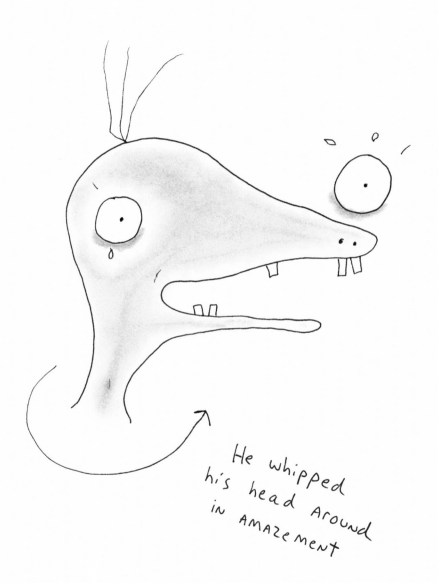

He whipped
his head Around
in AMAZEMENT

But Carl was Silent

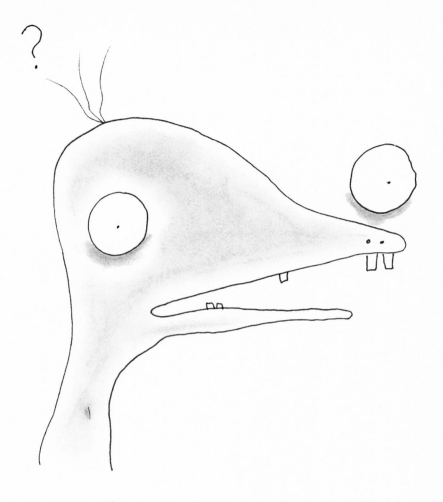

And then he heard
the same voice again...

A little bit louder
this time

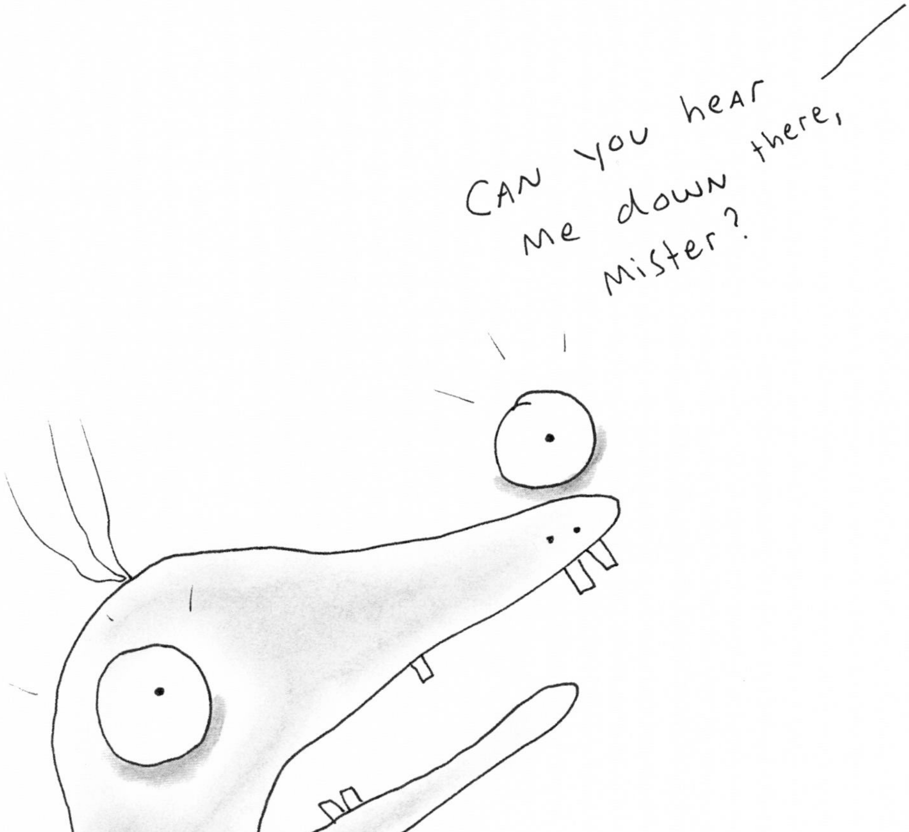
CAN you hear me down there, Mister?

the voice wasn't coming
from Candy Corn Carl,
it was coming from
the rain drain!

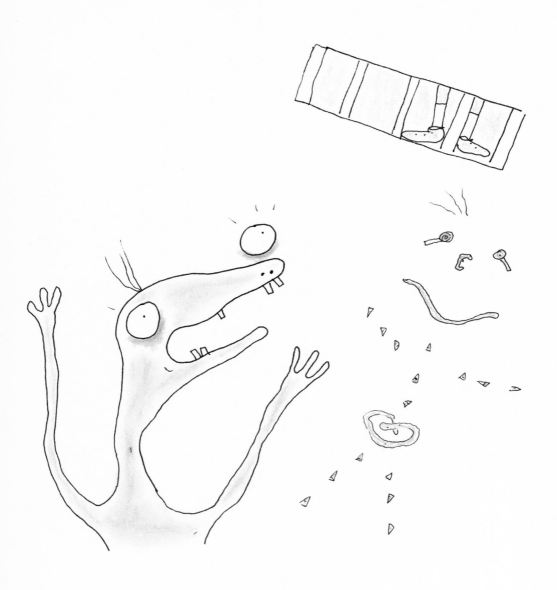

Sorry to bother you, but we were just wondering if you were going to watch the parade this year?

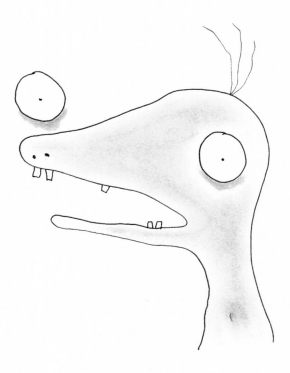

Rumple sheepishly replied...

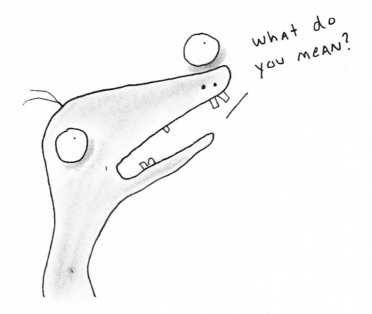

what do
you mean?

of course
we CAN see you
you're kind of
hard to miss

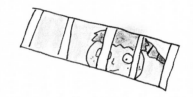

But Aren't you scared of me?

then

A different voice replied...

Because I have 5
crooked teeth
3 strands of hair
Green scaly skin
and my left foot
is slightly bigger
than my right...

I'm weird

"Well, look at me!"
Replied the boy. "I have really
big cheeks, metal on my teeth,
and my entire body is covered
in freckles."

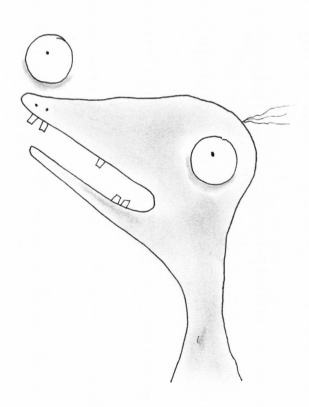

"And look at me!
I have really thick
glasses, a super pointy
nose, and can't
pwonounce the letter R!"

All of a sudden, Rumple
didn't feel so Alone

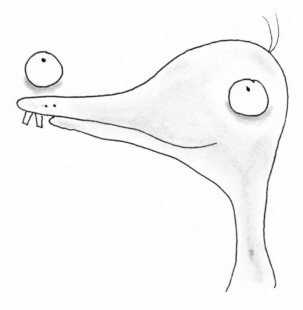

He moved closer to
the rain drain, got up
on his tiptoes, looked
out and saw...

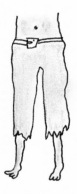

tip toes

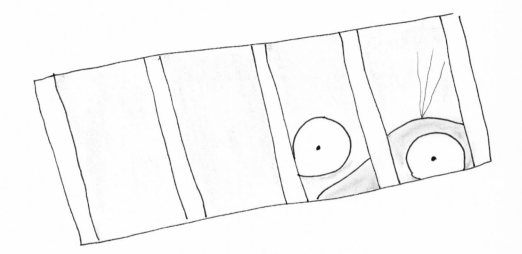

And that's when Rumple Realized...

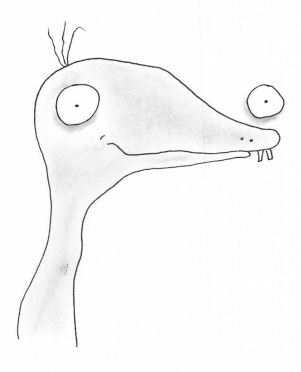

Everyone is weird

and that's what
MAKes us great

Pulling Rumple above ground,
the boy remarked...

OH NO!
thought Rumple...
"WHAT?"

why do you
Always wear
A bANANA peel
On your head?

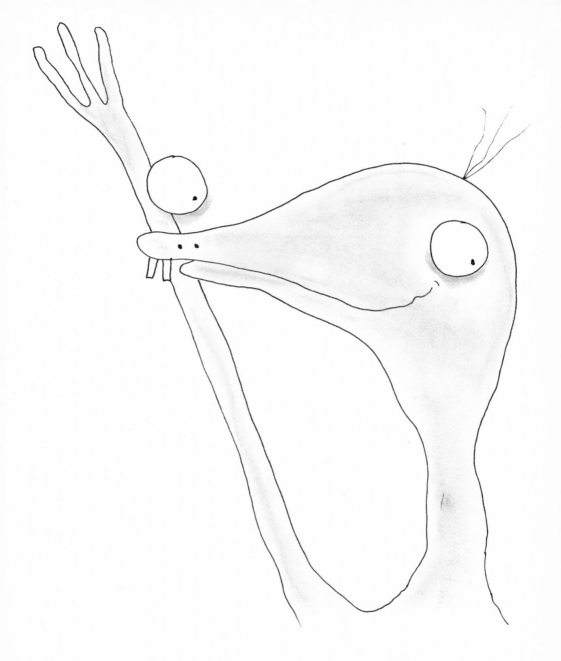

And Rumple just smiled

All this time they could
See him After all And Nobody
cared that he had
5 crooked teeth
3 strands of hair
Green scaly skin
or even A BANANA peel
on his head!

And the town was so
happy their new friend had
decided to join them above
ground they insisted he
lead the parade from on
top of the highest
float

High up there Above ground,
wAy higher than he had
   ever been before, Rumple
could feel the wind in
   his 3 strands
   of hair

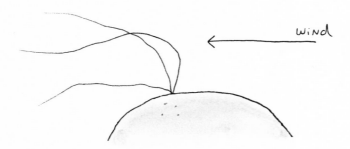

wind

He could taste
the cotton candy
PANCAKES iN his
5 crooked teeth

SUN

And he could finally feel the warm welcoming sun beating down on his green scaly skin

But the warmest
feeling of all he felt on
the inside

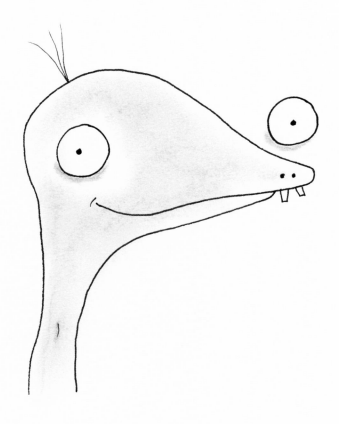

Knowing he was surrounded
by all his new friends

who . . .

All wore BANANA peels on
their heads in honor of their
Newest friend, Rumple Buttercup

the End

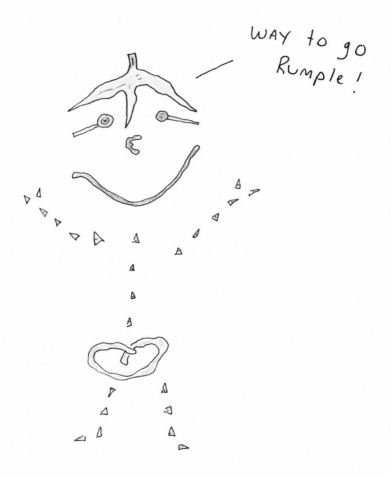

ABout the AuthoR

Matthew Gray Gubler writes, directs,
paints, acts, and knows magic. He
has a squeaky left knee, the posture
of an earthworm, and he looks
like a noodle when he dances.
this is his first book and
he wrote it just
for you!

for more information you can
find him in his pillow fort or at:

matthewgraygubler.com

 @ GuBLERNATION

@ Gublergram